This edition published by Kids Can Press in 2016

First edition 2015, published in French under the title *Lucie et cie*.
Published with the permission of Comme des géants inc.
6504, av Christophe-Colomb, Montreal (Quebec) H2S 2G8

Text and illustrations © 2015 Marianne Dubuc
Translation rights arranged through VeroK Agency, Spain
English translation © Kids Can Press

Kids Can Press acknowledges the financial support of the
Government of Ontario, through the Ontario Media Development
Corporation's Ontario Book Initiative; the Ontario Arts Council;
the Canada Council for the Arts; and the Government of Canada,
through the CBF, for our publishing activity.

Published in Canada by   Published in the U.S. by
Kids Can Press Ltd.   Kids Can Press Ltd.
25 Dockside Drive   2250 Military Road
Toronto, ON M5A 0B5   Tonawanda, NY 14150

www.kidscanpress.com

Original edition edited by Nadine Robert and Mathieu Lavoie
English edition edited by Yvette Ghione
Designed by Mathieu Lavoie

This book is smyth sewn casebound.
Manufactured in Malaysia in 3/2016 by Tien Wah Press (Pte.) Ltd.

CM 16 0 9 8 7 6 5 4 3 2 1

Library and Archives Canada Cataloguing in Publication

Dubuc, Marianne, 1980–
[Lucie et cie. English]
   Lucy and company / Marianne Dubuc.

Translation of: Lucie et cie.
ISBN 978-1-77138-662-3 (hardback)

   I. Title. II. Title: Lucie et cie. English.

PS8607.U2245L8213 2016   jC843'.6   C2016-900179-2

Kids Can Press is a *l'©rus*™ Entertainment company

LUCY & COMPANY

marianne dubuc

KIDS CAN PRESS

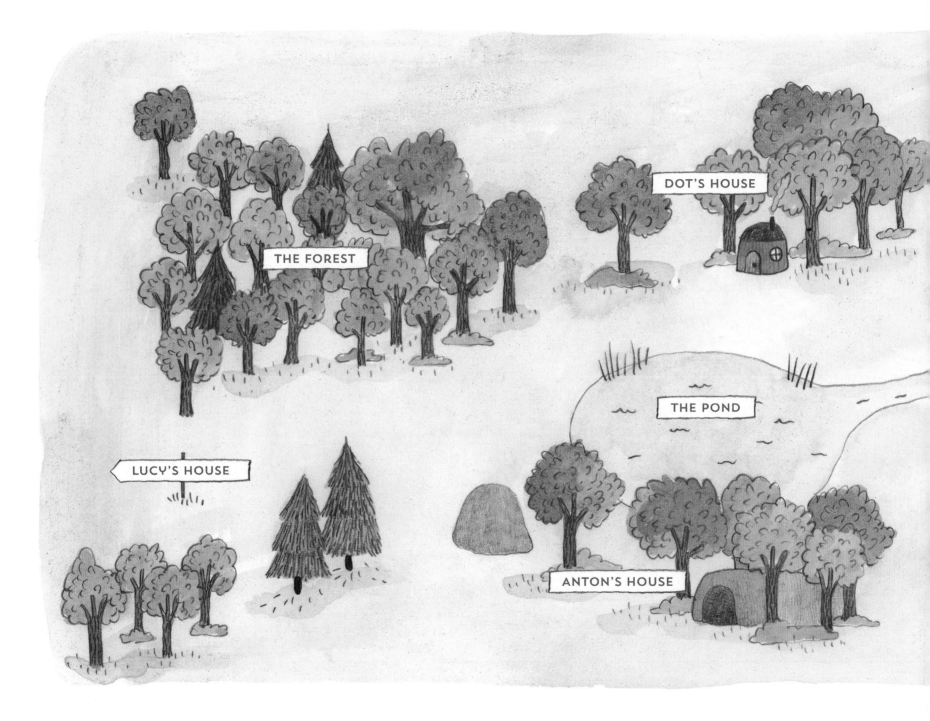

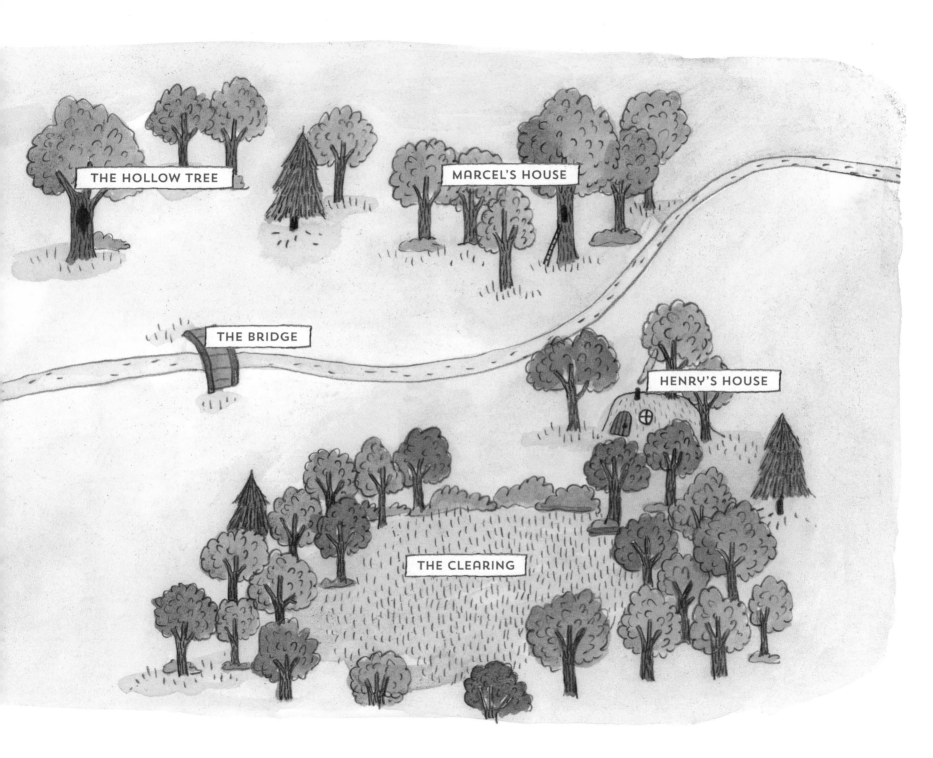

The Snack

Lucy is looking for a special spot to have her snack.

This branch is perfect.
"What a wonderful view."

Look — it's Marcel!
"Can I sit with you?"

Lucy unwraps her snack. "Mmmm ... strawberry biscuits."
Marcel only has a lettuce sandwich.

"Here comes Henry!"
Lucy and Marcel invite him to join them on their branch.

"I have hazelnuts. Would you like some?" asks Henry.

"Hey, Dot! Come and join us!"
say the three friends, high up in the tree.

"I lost my snack," explains poor Dot. "It fell into the
river when I was crossing the bridge."

Lucy offers Dot a biscuit, and Henry gives her some hazelnuts. Sharing snack time with friends is a real treat!

Suddenly one of Henry's hazelnuts shouts,
"NOOOO! Don't eat me!"

It isn't a nut!
"What are you?" asks Marcel.
"He's cute," says Lucy.

"My name is Adrian and I am HUNGRY!"
says the nut, which is in fact a snail.

But there is nothing left to eat.
"We dropped it all," sigh Lucy, Dot and Henry.
"Everything except my lettuce sandwich!" says Marcel.

Sharing snack time with a new friend is a real treat!

The Treasure Hunt

Lucy has found a treasure map.

"Hi, Lucy!" says Henry.
"What are you doing?" the others ask her.

"I'm looking for the treasure buried under this big red X. According to the map, I need to walk in the direction of the hollow tree."

"Wait for us, Lucy!" shout the four friends, leaving their game behind.

At the pond, they need to take five steps to the left.

"Henry steps or Marcel steps?" asks Adrian, who doesn't take steps.

They take Dot steps — not too big, not too small. 1 … 2 … 3 … 4 …

... 5! Next, they need to cross the bridge.

"According to the map, the treasure should be behind this rock," says Lucy.
"Oh!" cries Marcel. "That isn't a rock at all!"

It's Anton! And Anton should *never* be disturbed.
"Sorry, Mr. B-B-Bear," stammers Lucy.

Phew! The friends had a lucky escape.
"Here is your rock, Lucy!" says Marcel. This time it's a real one.

Time to get digging.
"After you, Henry!" says Lucy.

Henry digs and digs and digs some more.
"Do you see anything?" his friends ask.

And Henry digs up ... a present!
"SURRRPRIIISE!" shout Lucy, Dot, Marcel and Adrian.
Today is Henry's birthday.

"Thank you for my birthday treasure!" says Henry.

The Hatchlings

Adrian has found three large eggs.

"Are they yours?" asks Lucy.
"Oh, no! Snail eggs aren't that big," says Adrian.

Adrian tries to brood the eggs, but something doesn't seem quite right.

"You should do it!" says Adrian.
Lucy gives it a try.

"OUCH!" Lucy cries with a jump. Something pricked her bottom!

Three sharp-beaked baby birds break out of their shells.
"MAMA!" the hatchlings chirp when they see Adrian.

"They think you're their mother," says Lucy.

From then on, the baby birds follow Adrian everywhere.

But one day — "ACHOO!" One of the babies sneezes.

"Adrian, hatchlings need to be kept warm," says Lucy.

Lucy and the others search high and low for a cozy
nook for them in the forest.

And they find just the spot. "Here is some soft,
warm moss for the babies, Adrian!"

"Who DARES wake me up?" growls a voice.
Uh-oh! It's Anton!

"PAPA!" chirp the hatchlings.
Anton is so surprised that he stops grumbling.

Shhhh! Quiet, please.
The hatchlings, cozy and warm, are asleep.
Sweet dreams!